Space Dog and Roy

by Natalie Standiford
illustrated by Kathleen Collins Howell

A STEPPING STONE BOOK™

Random House  New York

For my mother and father

http://www.randomhouse.com/

Library of Congress Cataloging-in-Publication Data
Standiford, Natalie.
Space Dog and Roy / by Natalie Standiford ; illustrated by Kathleen Collins Howell.
p. cm. "A Stepping Stone book." SUMMARY: Roy, who has always wanted a dog,
thinks he's found the perfect pet when an explorer from the planet Queekrg, whose
inhabitants are all dogs, crash-lands in the backyard.
ISBN 0-679-88903-5 (pbk.) — ISBN 0-679-98903-X (lib. bdg.)
[1. Dogs—Fiction. 2. Pets—Fiction. 3. Extraterrestrial beings—Fiction.]
 I. Howell, Kathleen Collins, ill. II. Title. PZ7.S78627Sp 1998 [Fic]—dc21
97-15560

Printed in the United States of America 10 9 8 7 6 5 4 3 2 1

A STEPPING STONE BOOK is a trademark of Random House, Inc.

Contents

1

Roy Wants a Dog

It was a cold and cloudy Saturday. Roy Barnes was sitting in the house, staring out a window. Roy was a regular-looking kid, with blue eyes, freckles, and a friendly face. But that day his blue eyes were cloudy with worry.

Roy was thinking about Stanley Moore, the school bully. Stanley had been picking on Roy a lot lately. He picked on Roy more than anyone else. It had gotten so bad that Roy didn't like school anymore. It was all Stanley's fault.

The doorbell rang. Roy answered it. There stood Roy's friend Alice. Alice lived next door. "Meet Blanche, my new dog," she said, pulling a curly black poodle around in front of her.

"Wow!" said Roy. "Where did you get her?"

"She was my aunt's," said Alice, leading Blanche into the house. "My aunt moved to a building where they can't have dogs. She had to give Blanche away. My mom said we could take her."

"Boy, are you lucky," said Roy. "I wish I had a dog. If I had a big German shepherd, Stanley wouldn't pick on me anymore." He bent down to pet Blanche. Blanche licked his fingers.

Alice straightened the little bow on Blanche's head. "Maybe your parents will get you a dog when they see how nice

Blanche is," said Alice. "In fact, Blanche is neater than I am." Alice did have a way of looking a little messy.

"My parents?" said Roy. "Get me a dog? No way."

Suddenly they heard a loud noise. It came from upstairs. It sounded like an explosion.

"Uh-oh," said Roy.

"What was that?" asked Alice.

The noise came again. Then a loud voice boomed, "Why am I sneezing? Is there a DOG in this house?"

"See?" said Roy. "My dad's allergic to dogs. Really allergic."

"I'd better get Blanche out of here," said Alice.

It was too late. Roy's father came downstairs. Mrs. Barnes was right behind him.

Mr. Barnes saw Blanche. "Get that DOG out of the house, Alice!" yelled Mr. Barnes. *"Aaaaah-CHOOOO!"*

"See you, Roy," said Alice. She yanked the poodle out the door as fast as she could.

When Blanche was gone, Mr. Barnes stopped sneezing. "For heaven's sake, Roy," said Mr. Barnes. "You know better than to let a dog in the house."

"I'm sorry," said Roy. "I forgot."

"Don't let it happen again, son," said Mr. Barnes. Then he turned to his wife. "Honey, is there any more Kleenex in the house?"

"I'll get it for you, dear," said Mrs. Barnes. "Roy, why don't you go outside and play?"

Roy looked out the window. "I can't," he said. "It's raining."

Roy went up to his room. He sat on the bottom of his double-decker bed and took out his new library book. The book was called *How to Take Care of Your Dog*.

2

Roy Has a Weird Feeling

That night, Roy lay awake for a long time. The skies had cleared. Moonbeams floated like ghosts through the bedroom window. Roy felt strange and tingly. *Something weird is going to happen*, he thought.

Suddenly he heard a noise outside. It sounded like a crash. He went to the window and looked out at the backyard.

He could see things clearly in the moonlight. There was a small heap of metal sitting in the yard. It looked like a mangled little spaceship. Roy watched as somebody climbed out of it—dressed in a spacesuit.

The creature took off its helmet. Roy thought he was dreaming. The space creature looked like a dog!

"Wow!" said Roy. He pinched himself hard to make sure he wasn't asleep.

The dog was standing up like a person. It looked at the spaceship and shook its head. Then it reached into a pocket and pulled out something that looked like a map.

Roy couldn't believe his eyes. Finally he pulled himself away from the window and ran downstairs for a closer look.

Roy tiptoed out the back door. Then he ran behind a bush. He could see that the dog was about his height. It had big ears and shaggy gray-and-white fur.

The dog seemed to know Roy was there. "Friend or foe?" it called.

Roy was scared. He didn't know what to do. He stayed behind the bush.

The dog sat down and started tugging at his space boots. "Hey, could you give me a hand here?" it said. "My feet are killing me."

Roy came out from behind the bush. He walked over and helped pull off the dog's boots.

"Who are you?" Roy asked.

"I am an explorer from the planet Queekrg," said the dog. "I'm on a scouting mission to Earth. It was supposed to be a secret mission."

"I won't tell anybody," said Roy.

"Thanks," said the dog. He held out his paw. Roy shook it.

"Wow," said Roy. "Are you really from

outer space? Can I call you 'Space Dog'?"

"I'm not a dog. I'm a citizen of Queekrg," said the dog. "And I already have a name. It's Qrxztlq."

Roy gave the dog a funny look.

"Okay," said the dog. "Call me Space Dog."

"My name is Roy," said Roy. "It's nice to meet you."

Space Dog looked sadly at his ship. "What a mess," he said.

"Can you fix it?" asked Roy.

"Of course," said the dog. "But I'll need some time."

"Why don't you live here while you work on it?" said Roy. "I've always wanted a dog."

"That's nice of you," said Space Dog. The dog looked at the white-painted house behind Roy. It was old-fashioned, but it would do.

First they had to hide the spaceship. Roy and Space Dog dragged it into the basement. They tried to be quiet so Roy's parents wouldn't wake up.

"Oh, my gosh!" Roy suddenly whispered. "You can't live here. My father is allergic to dogs!"

"I'm not a dog," said Space Dog, "so your father probably won't be allergic to me."

"I hope you're right," said Roy. "Anyway, we'll find out pretty fast."

By then it was very late. Roy yawned. "I'm sleepy."

Space Dog yawned, too. "Let's hit the hay," he said.

They tiptoed upstairs to Roy's room. They went inside and closed the door.

At last Roy had a dog! He emptied the

laundry basket and put a pillow in it. "You can sleep here," he told Space Dog.

But Space Dog had already climbed up to the top bunk of Roy's bed.

"Queekrites don't sleep in baskets," he said. "They sleep in beds."

"Okay," said Roy. "But you'll have to sleep on the bottom. *I* sleep on the top."

"All right," said Space Dog. "As long as it's a bed. I'm pooped."

"Me too," said Roy. Space Dog settled into the bottom bunk, and Roy climbed into the top.

"Good night, Roy," said Space Dog.

"Good night, Space Dog," said Roy. "I sure am glad you crashed in my backyard."

3

Space Dog Joins the Family

The next day was Sunday. When Roy woke up, he heard someone snoring down below. He leaned over and saw Space Dog.

It wasn't a dream, thought Roy. *I really do have a dog.*

While Space Dog slept, Roy went downstairs. He smelled sausage. His mother was in the kitchen, making pancakes.

"Good morning, Roy," said Mrs. Barnes.

"Good morning, Mom," said Roy. "Guess what?"

"What?"

Roy stopped. He didn't know what to say next. How could he tell his mother about Space Dog?

"Roy?" said Mrs. Barnes. "What were you going to tell me?"

"Well," said Roy. "I, uh, found a dog. A really great dog! Can I keep him?"

"A dog?" said Mrs. Barnes. "Where is he now?"

"Up in my room," said Roy. "He slept there last night, and he was really good. He didn't chew up a single thing!"

"Oh, Roy," said Mrs. Barnes. "You know I'd love to have a dog. But with your father's allergies…"

"This dog isn't like other dogs," said Roy. "Wait till you see him, Mom. I'll bring him downstairs."

Roy ran to his room. Space Dog was

still asleep. "Wake up!" said Roy. "Come meet my mom."

Space Dog snorted and lifted his head. "Huh?" he grumbled. "Where am I?"

Roy shook him. "Come on!" he said.

Space Dog sat up. "Whatever's cooking sure smells good."

"That's pancakes and sausage," said Roy. "But you can't eat stuff like that. You have to eat dog food."

"I know a lot about Earth," said Space Dog. "But I don't know anything about dog food." He stood up and added, "Could I borrow a bathrobe, Roy?"

"No!" said Roy. "Dogs don't wear bathrobes!"

"Well, could I borrow a sweater, then?"

"Dogs don't wear any clothes at all," said Roy.

"What do they do, walk around naked?"

Roy looked serious. "Listen, Space Dog," he said. "You *have* to act like a dog. When you meet my mom, you have to walk on four legs, like this." Roy got down on his hands and knees.

Space Dog laughed. "Are you kidding?" he said. "That looks silly."

"Trust me, Space Dog. You don't want them to know about your secret mission, do you?"

"No," said Space Dog. "But I don't want to look like a fool either. Crawling on all fours, naked!"

"Space Dog, this is important," said Roy. "If anyone learns you came from outer space, that will be the end of your secret mission."

Space Dog perked up his ears.

"Scientists will come and take you away," said Roy. "Then they will study you, maybe even take your brain apart or something."

Space Dog sighed. He got down and tried to walk on four legs. He wobbled, but he managed it.

They started down the stairs. "Wag your tail, too," Roy whispered. "And maybe lick my mom's hand or something."

"That's disgusting," said Space Dog.

At last they reached the kitchen.

"Mom," said Roy, "meet Space Dog!"

"Space Dog?" said Mrs. Barnes. "That's a funny name." She patted Space Dog on the head. Space Dog tried to wag his tail. It looked as if he was doing the hokey-pokey.

"Is he hurt?" asked Mrs. Barnes. "He isn't wagging his tail right."

Just then they heard a big, loud yawn. It sounded like feeding time at the zoo.

"Uh-oh," said Mrs. Barnes. "Your dad is coming. Hide the dog, quick! Put him in the pantry!"

Roy shoved Space Dog into the pantry and closed the door.

"Hey, Roy!" Space Dog called from the pantry.

"What was that, Roy?" said Mrs. Barnes.

"Nothing, Mom," said Roy. "Probably just Dad."

Just then, Mr. Barnes walked into the kitchen. "Goo-o-od morning!" he said. He took a deep breath and patted his chest. "Ah, it's a great spring day!"

Roy and his mom looked at each other. They waited for Mr. Barnes to sneeze. But nothing happened.

"Do I smell sausage?" said Mr. Barnes.

"Yes, dear," said Mrs. Barnes. "And pancakes. They're almost ready. Sit down and have some coffee."

Roy and his dad sat down. Mrs. Barnes served breakfast. Everyone started to eat.

"Delicious, honey," said Mr. Barnes.

Suddenly they heard someone knocking. It came from the pantry. Roy and his mother looked at each other.

"What was that?" said Mr. Barnes.

"I didn't hear anything," said Mrs. Barnes.

"Me either," said Roy.

But they heard the knocking again.

"I guess someone's at the back door," said Mrs. Barnes.

"Someone is at the *pantry* door," said Mr. Barnes. "And I'm going to find out who!" He got up and walked toward the pantry.

"Don't go in there, honey," said Mrs.

Barnes. "No one's in the pantry."

But there was more knocking.

"Someone *is* in the pantry!" said Mr. Barnes.

He opened the pantry door wide. Space Dog bounded out.

"A DOG!" shouted Mr. Barnes. "What is a DOG doing in the pantry? What about MY ALLERGIES!"

"But, Dad," said Roy. "You're not sneezing."

Mr. Barnes stopped shouting. He took a little sniff of air.

He took a bigger sniff.

He leaned down and put his nose in Space Dog's fur and sniffed.

He didn't sneeze. His eyes didn't water!

"Hey," cried Mr. Barnes. "Maybe I'm not allergic to this dog!"

Roy and Mrs. Barnes clapped. "Hurray!" said Roy.

"Where did he come from?" asked Mr. Barnes.

"I think he's a stray," said Roy. "I heard him in the backyard last night. I went down and let him in. He has no collar. Can I keep him, Dad?"

"Well, I guess so," said Mr. Barnes, "if I don't start sneezing. Have you thought of a name?"

"Space Dog," said Roy.

"Space Dog?" repeated Mr. Barnes.

4

Dog Training

"After breakfast, we'll go get some dog food," Mr. Barnes told Roy. "And a collar and a leash."

"Great, Dad," said Roy. "But in the meantime, could I give Space Dog some pancakes?"

"I don't think dogs like pancakes, son," said Mr. Barnes.

"Maybe Space Dog does," said Roy.

"Okay," said Mr. Barnes. "Let's give it a shot."

Space Dog jumped up into an empty chair. He waited eagerly for his breakfast.

"Oh, no you don't, pooch," said Mr. Barnes. "Down, boy." He put a plate of pancakes on the floor.

Roy sat down next to Space Dog. "Sorry," he whispered.

"Meet me in the living room, pronto," Space Dog whispered back. He trotted out of the kitchen without touching the pancakes.

Roy stood up. "I'll be right back," he told his parents. Then he left the kitchen, too.

"There's something strange about that dog," said Mr. Barnes.

"I know what you mean, dear," said Mrs. Barnes. "But Roy likes him."

Roy went into the living room. He found

Space Dog sitting on the sofa.

"What's the story here, Roy?" said Space Dog. "Eating off the floor? Pancakes without syrup? And a man who calls me *pooch?*"

"I'm really sorry," said Roy. "But that's how dogs live. They don't mind being treated that way."

"Earth dogs must be stupid," said Space Dog.

"They're not stupid," said Roy. "They're just not like you."

Space Dog sighed. "I'll have to get used to a dog's life, I guess. But it's confusing! I learned all about Earth people for this mission. I knew they weren't as advanced as Queekrites. But I didn't know I would have to behave like—like an animal!"

Roy looked unhappy. "A dog isn't just

as usual. Her socks were falling down. The bow on her braid was untied.

"I'm teaching my new dog some tricks," said Roy.

"Your new dog?" said Alice. "But your father's allergic to dogs."

"He's not allergic to *this* one," said Roy. "Alice, meet Space Dog."

Space Dog was polite and stuck out his paw.

"Oh!" said Alice, shaking Space Dog's paw. "He already knows how to shake! But he's sort of funny-looking. What breed is he?"

"Uh, he's a mutt," said Roy.

Space Dog glared at Roy. A mutt indeed!

Then Blanche walked over to Space Dog. She started sniffing his face. Space Dog wanted to say, "Get away from me!"

any old animal," he said. "He's man's best friend! Everyone loves dogs. You'll see."

After breakfast, Roy and his father drove to a pet store. As soon as they came back, Roy dragged Space Dog out to the backyard. He wanted to start Space Dog's training program.

Roy took out the collar and put it around Space Dog's neck. Space Dog pulled away. "What do you think you're doing?" he demanded.

"The collar has our name and address on it," said Roy. "You need it in case you get lost."

"I'm not going to get lost," said Space Dog. "And if I do, I'll just call you on the phone. I know all about telephones."

"But what if somebody sees you making a call?" said Roy.

"Hmm, I see your point," said Space Dog. "Okay, go on."

"This is your leash," said Roy. "You have to be on a leash when I take you for a walk."

"Why?"

"It's the town law," said Roy. "All dogs have to be on leashes. Or the dogcatcher will get you."

"The dogcatcher?"

"He'll take you to the dog pound and lock you up," Roy explained. "It's like jail."

"This dog's life is getting worse," said Space Dog.

"Now," said Roy, holding up an old tennis ball. "Here's your ball. You can chew on it if you want to."

"No, thank you," said Space Dog.

"I'll throw it, like this." Roy tossed the ball across the yard. "Now you run over, pick it up, and bring it back to me."

Space Dog looked at Roy blankly.

"Go ahead," said Roy.

Space Dog wobbled over to the ball on four legs. Then he picked it up in one paw and tossed it back to Roy.

"No, no, no!" said Roy. "Pick it up in your mouth. You're not supposed to be able to throw!"

"But I *am* able!" Space Dog insisted.

"I know," said Roy. "But you have to do what I say. I'm your master."

Space Dog looked sad. "I thought you were my friend," he said.

Suddenly Roy felt sorry. "I *am* your friend," he said. "Forget about that master stuff. But please, will you act like a dog?"

Roy tossed the ball again. This time, Space Dog picked it up in his mouth, trotted over to Roy, and dropped it at his feet.

"Good," said Roy. "You're getting the hang of it."

Just then, Roy heard a voice call, "Hey, Roy!" It was Alice. And she had Blanche with her. They came into Roy's yard. Blanche looked fine, but Alice was a mess,

But he knew he couldn't—not in front of Alice.

"Look at Blanche!" said Alice. "She likes your dog."

"Well, I don't think Space Dog likes Blanche," said Roy. He shooed Blanche away from Space Dog.

Thank you, Roy, thought Space Dog. He looked at Blanche. She was slobbering. *What a dopey face*, thought Space Dog. *I hope she won't come around too much.*

"Go away now, Alice," said Roy. "Space Dog and I have work to do."

"Blanche and I want to watch," said Alice. She pushed her glasses up on her nose. "Don't we, Blanche?"

Blanche wagged her tail. Her tongue hung out. She slobbered on the grass. Space Dog could hardly stand looking at her.

Then Alice picked up the ball. "Look what Blanche can do," she said.

Alice tossed the ball. Blanche ran after it. She picked it up in her mouth and brought it back to Alice.

"Can Space Dog do that?" asked Alice.

"Sure he can," said Roy. He took the ball from Alice. He tossed it across the yard. Space Dog walked after it. When he reached the ball, he stopped. The ball was all slobbery from Blanche's mouth.

Space Dog turned around and looked at Roy.

"Go ahead, Space Dog," said Roy. "Pick up the ball."

Space Dog was *not* going to pick up the ball. He stared at Roy harder.

Roy walked up to him. "What's the matter?" he whispered.

"The ball is all slobbery," mumbled

Space Dog. "I will *not* put it in my mouth."

"But Alice is watching!" said Roy. Roy looked back at Alice.

"Well?" said Alice.

"Well, nothing," said Roy. "Space Dog is just tired."

"Sure," said Alice. "Well, Blanchie and I have to go home now. I want to give her a cookie for being so smart."

Off they went. Blanche wagged her tail proudly, like a real dog.

5

Space Dog Tries Dog Food

After lunch, Roy started building a dog-house. He got some wood and nails from the basement. Space Dog told him what to do. The doghouse was going to be Space Dog's secret workshop. Inside he would do research about Earth.

All afternoon Roy hammered away. Space Dog wanted to help. But Roy wouldn't let him. Roy said it would look funny to see a dog building his own house.

"Besides, I don't mind," said Roy. "I've

always wanted a doghouse in the backyard."

"When I was a young—uh—puppy,"
said Space Dog, "I wanted a pet fish."

"A fish?" said Roy, looking up from his
work. "Fish are boring."

"On my planet they swim through air
instead of water, so they can go anywhere.
They're fun."

"Flying fish!" said Roy. "Cool."

"I wanted a fish very badly," said Space
Dog. "But my mother didn't want fish
scales all over the furniture."

"Did you ever get one?" asked Roy
between hammerings. "A fish, I mean."

"Well, I found a stray one day. I named
him Zexl and took him home."

"Oh, no," said Roy. "What did your
mom say?"

"She took one look and said, 'Get that

mangy fish out of here!'" said Space Dog. "Then Zexl whined a little, like this: 'Yee yee yee.' He sounded hungry. He looked at my mother with his big, sad, fishy eyes. Finally my mother said I could feed him before I let him go."

Roy was not hammering anymore. "*Then* what happened?" he asked.

"I gave Zexl some freeze-dried qixzit powder. But he wouldn't eat it. Mom said I wasn't doing it right. Then she fed him, and Zexl ate right out of her hand. Mom stopped telling me to get rid of him. Zexl lived with us a long time."

"That's a good story," said Roy. "I liked the last part best."

He began to hammer again.

By the end of the day, the doghouse was finished—except for the roof.

Roy sat back on the grass. "A roof is hard to build," he said. "Maybe we can find some canvas to go over the top."

"Sure," said Space Dog. "Roy, I like my new place a lot. Thank you."

Just then, Roy's mother opened the back door. "That is some doghouse," she said. And it was. It was bigger than most. It looked like a playhouse.

"Come in for supper," said Mrs. Barnes. "We sent out for a surprise."

"Let's go!" whispered Space Dog. "I'm hungry."

"Wait a minute," said Roy. "You're going to have to eat dog food tonight, you know. My dad bought some for you."

"What's it like?" asked Space Dog.

"It's like stew, I guess," said Roy. "Just remember, you have to eat it with your mouth, not your paws."

"Yes, yes," said Space Dog. "Let's go inside."

They went into the house. Mrs. Barnes was already at the table. Mr. Barnes was opening a big, flat box. Pizza! It smelled great.

Roy sat at the table. Space Dog sat nearby on the floor. Mr. Barnes said, "Hey there, pooch. I'll get you some supper. I almost forgot about you."

Space Dog hoped it wouldn't be dog food after all. The dripping pizza looked delicious.

But Mr. Barnes didn't cut a slice of pizza for Space Dog. He opened a can of dog food instead. Then he plopped some brown stuff into a plastic bowl and set it on the floor.

"There you go, pooch," he said.

Space Dog looked at the food. It didn't

look good, but he was too hungry to argue. He took a big bite.

Roy was watching when Space Dog suddenly froze. His mouth was full, but he didn't chew. Then he spit the food out on the floor and ran out of the room.

"Space Dog! Wait!" called Roy. "It's just dog food." He followed him out of the kitchen. But Space Dog ran upstairs to Roy's room and slammed the door.

"Hey! That dog just threw up on the floor!" said Mr. Barnes angrily. "Roy! You get back here and clean this up!"

Roy went back to the kitchen.

"Take the dog outside," said Mr. Barnes. "He might throw up again."

"He didn't throw up, Dad," said Roy. "He just doesn't like dog food." Roy bent down to clean up the mess.

"Doesn't like dog food! Well, that's

just too bad," said Mr. Barnes. "He's a dog, isn't he? So he eats dog food. I will not have a dog running this house."

"But, Dad..." said Roy.

"That's final," said Mr. Barnes.

Roy ate his supper in silence. He was worried about Space Dog. There were a lot of things about being an Earth dog that seemed to make Space Dog unhappy. Roy was afraid he wouldn't have a dog very long. Space Dog might really leave.

After supper, Roy helped his father clean up. Then they turned on the dishwasher, and his father went into the living room.

Roy was alone in the kitchen at last. There were two pieces of leftover pizza. He put them in a napkin and sneaked upstairs to his room. Space Dog was lying under the covers. He was reading *How to*

Take Care of Your Dog.

"I'm checking out the part about feeding," he said. "Everything in this chapter sounds awful."

"Here," said Roy. "I brought you some pizza."

Space Dog took the napkin. He unwrapped the pizza. "It's cold," he said.

"I'm sorry," said Roy. "But I couldn't heat it up. I'm not allowed to use the oven."

"That's okay," said Space Dog. "I'll eat it cold."

They sat on the bed together while Space Dog munched on the pizza. Then there was a knock at the door.

"Quick! Hide the pizza!" said Roy.

Space Dog put it under his pillow. Roy called, "Come in."

It was his mother. "Bedtime, Roy. You

have school tomorrow," she said. She reached over for Space Dog. "That dog shouldn't be on your bed," she said.

"He's fine, Mom," said Roy. "I told him he could sleep there."

Mrs. Barnes shook her head. "Honestly, Roy," she said. "Ever since that dog appeared you've been acting strangely. Now get ready for bed. I'll come back to kiss you good night."

When Mrs. Barnes left the room, Space Dog pulled his pizza out from under the pillow.

"Don't let my mom see that pillow-case," said Roy.

"Oh, sorry," said Space Dog.

"That's okay," said Roy. "Maybe I can wash off the pizza tomorrow."

Roy put on his pajamas. Then Mr. and Mrs. Barnes came in and kissed him good night.

The lights were out. Space Dog's pillow smelled of cheese and tomato. He couldn't sleep.

Maybe I don't like being an Earth dog, thought Space Dog. *The food is lousy. Maybe I should start fixing my spaceship tomorrow. Then I'll be able to go home. Who wants to study a dumpy old planet like Earth anyway?*

Roy was also tossing and turning.

Having a dog is great, he thought. *But it's harder than I thought it would be. Whoever heard of a dog that has to learn to be a dog? I just hope he doesn't hate it here. If he does, he'll leave!*

It was a hard night for both of them. At last they fell asleep.

6

Roy Has a Bad Day

The next morning, Roy's alarm clock woke Space Dog. It didn't wake Roy. Space Dog poked the bed above him. "Hey, Roy! Wake up!"

Roy turned off the alarm, but he had trouble getting out of bed. Finally he stumbled into the bathroom. He didn't want to go to school. Stanley the bully would be there waiting for him.

Space Dog went downstairs. The front door was open. He saw the newspaper on the steps outside. He went out and picked up the paper—in his mouth.

Space Dog carried the paper into the kitchen. Mr. Barnes was at the kitchen table, drinking coffee. He saw Space Dog with the newspaper.

"Good dog!" said Mr. Barnes. "You've brought me the paper!"

But Space Dog walked right past Mr. Barnes and kept on going—out the back door to his doghouse. He wanted the newspaper for his research.

"Hey!" shouted Mr. Barnes. "Bring back my paper!" He followed Space Dog outside.

Roy heard the shouting. He ran downstairs and out into the yard to see what was happening.

"Roy!" said Mr. Barnes. "Your dog stole my paper! He's in that doghouse. I bet he's tearing it up."

"I bet he's reading it," said Roy.

"Don't joke with me, young man," said Mr. Barnes.

Roy stuck his head in the doghouse. "Space Dog, give Dad his paper," he said. "You can have it after he's done."

Space Dog handed Roy the paper. Roy handed it to his father.

"Thank you," said Mr. Barnes. He marched back into the house.

"I have to go in to breakfast," Roy told Space Dog.

"What about me?" said Space Dog.

"I'll bring you some toast before I go to school. Bye."

"Bye, Roy," said Space Dog sadly.

Roy made it to school without running into Stanley the bully. That was good. He sat down at his desk and remembered math was the first subject. He was not good at math.

"Hi, Roy," said Alice. She had the desk next to Roy's. "How's your new dog?"

"He's fine," said Roy. "I just hope he's happy."

"Why wouldn't he be?" said Alice. "It doesn't take much to make a dog happy."

"That's what you think," said Roy.

Ms. Humphrey came in and told everyone to open his or her workbook to page thirty-nine. She told the class to do all the problems on that page.

Roy tried to multiply, but he couldn't keep his mind on math. He was thinking about Space Dog. Would he remember to act like a dog when Roy's mother was around? Would his mother force him to eat dog food?

"Roy? Roy?" said Ms. Humphrey. "I

want the answer to the first problem."

Roy sat up. "Um, the answer is seven," he said.

"Wrong, Roy," said Ms. Humphrey. "You'd better pay attention. We're having a test on this tomorrow."

Uh-oh, thought Roy. *This is turning into a bad day.*

At recess, Roy and Alice climbed on the monkey bars. Alice hung upside down. Roy held her glasses.

"Maybe Blanche and Space Dog will fall in love," said Alice. "Wouldn't that be great?"

"No, it wouldn't," said Roy. Alice was still upside down. Roy reached over for her braid. He tried to tie it in a knot.

"Stop it!" said Alice. "Blanche and Space Dog could get married and have

puppies. Then we would be related!"

"What a dumb idea," said Roy. "Dogs don't get married."

"At least they could play together while we're at school. I think Blanche gets lonely."

"Space Dog won't get lonely," said Roy. "He has things to do."

"What things?" said Alice, still in her upside-down position.

"Oh. Uh, things like digging holes in the backyard," said Roy.

Alice swung down from the monkey bars. Her face was flushed from being upside down. She walked over to the water fountain. Roy followed her. All of a sudden, he tripped and fell flat on his face.

"Ha ha ha!" laughed a big fat voice. It was big fat Stanley. He had tripped Roy on purpose.

"You leave him alone!" said Alice. She pushed up her glasses.

"How are you going to make me, Four-Eyes?" said Stanley.

"I'll sic my dog on you," said Alice.

"Oh! I'm scared, I'm scared!" said Stanley in a high, squeaky voice. "Your prissy little poodle is going to hurt me."

The bell rang. Roy brushed himself off. "Let's go, Alice," he said. They started to walk back into the school building.

"Look out this afternoon, Barnes!" Stanley called after Roy. "You might run into me on your way home from school."

"What a jerk," said Alice. "Don't worry, Roy. He's all bark and no bite."

"Sure," said Roy, but he wasn't sure at all.

7

Roy Is Scared

Roy was nervous all the way home from school. He was waiting for Stanley to strike. He glanced behind bushes and parked cars. He didn't see Stanley.

This is crazy, thought Roy. *I have to do something. Maybe Space Dog can help. After all, he is a dog. Sort of.*

When Roy got home, he went straight to the backyard. Space Dog was in his doghouse. He was working on something that looked like an engine.

"Hi, Roy," said Space Dog. "How was school?"

"Not great," said Roy. "I have a problem."

Space Dog put down his screwdriver. He offered Roy some cookies. He had taken them from the kitchen when Mrs. Barnes wasn't looking.

"What kind of problem?" asked Space Dog. "Math? I love math problems."

"It isn't a math problem," said Roy. "It's a bully problem. This boy named Stanley hates me. He says he's going to beat me up. He's very big, Space Dog."

"I know about bullies," said Space Dog. "On Queekrg I worked with a scientist named Tzaxette. She was big. She was mean. Every time I had a good idea, she punched me."

"What did you do?" asked Roy.

"I offered to go on this mission," said Space Dog. "It meant I could get away from her."

"That won't work for me," said Roy. "I have to go to school. I can't get out of it. I was thinking maybe you could help me."

"Me?" said Space Dog. "What can I do?"

"A lot of people are afraid of dogs," said Roy. "Maybe you could scare Stanley."

"How? If he's bigger than you, he's bigger than I am. He could beat me up."

"Not if you act mean," said Roy. "Try it. Show your teeth. Growl."

"Growl?" said Space Dog.

"Like this," said Roy. "*Grrr.* Now you try it."

Space Dog stuck out his lips and said, "Gerbil."

"Try again," said Roy. "*Grrr!*"

"Gurgle."

"No, no," said Roy. "*Grrr* isn't a word. It's a sound. Maybe Blanche should teach you."

"Not Blanche!" said Space Dog. "I don't want her near me."

"Try it once more," said Roy. "*Grrrrrr!*"

"Gir-r-r-r-dle!"

"I give up," said Roy. "No one's going to be scared of a dog who growls 'girdle.'"

"Sorry," said Space Dog.

Roy munched on a cookie for a minute, thinking. Then he said, "Maybe you don't need to growl. Maybe if Stanley just *sees* you, he'll be scared. Will you come to school with me tomorrow?"

"Great!" said Space Dog. "I would love to see an Earth school firsthand. Will I get to sit next to you?"

"Not exactly," said Roy. "You can't go in the building. We'll just walk to and from school together. In between you'll have to be tied up on the playground."

"So dogs can't go to school," said Space Dog. "No wonder Blanche seems so dumb."

"Will you do it?" asked Roy. "Will you walk to school with me?"

"No way," said Space Dog. "How would *you* like to be tied up all day?"

"I'd hate it," said Roy. "I guess I'll have to think of something else."

Space Dog knew he had let Roy down. He tried to make up for it. "Do you need any help with your homework?" he asked. "I'd be good at that."

Roy smiled. "No thanks," he said. Space Dog started working on the engine again.

"What's that?" asked Roy.

"The main engine from my spaceship.

I'm trying to fix it," said Space Dog.

"Oh," said Roy. "Well, I should go and tell Mom I'm home. See you later."

Roy went into the house. Then it hit him. Space Dog was working on his engine. That meant he *was* going to leave!

8

Space Dog to the Rescue

The next morning, Roy woke up with butterflies in his stomach. *Last week I only had one thing to worry about,* he thought. *That was Stanley. This week I have two things to worry about—Stanley and Space Dog.*

I have to get Space Dog to stay. I just have to!

Space Dog was still asleep. Roy listened to him snore. *He's a cute snorer,* Roy thought sadly.

Then the butterflies came back again.

Ugh, I have to go to school today, he thought. *I wish Stanley would move someplace else. Like Egypt.*

Roy forced himself to get dressed. Then he went downstairs to the kitchen. He drank his juice, but he didn't eat anything. He started off to school with a heavy heart.

Space Dog worked on his engine most of the day. It was a big job. He needed more time.

He took a break in the afternoon. He picked up the newspaper and turned to the funnies. Suddenly he felt someone watching him.

Space Dog looked up. Blanche stood in the door of the doghouse. She was panting and drooling.

"Oh, no," said Space Dog. "Not you

again."

Blanche started nosing her way farther into the doghouse.

"Go away!" said Space Dog. "I'm busy."

Blanche whined. She stuck her drooly snout closer. She tried to lick his ear.

"Scat!" said Space Dog. "This place is top-secret!" He pushed Blanche out of the doghouse, but she came right back in. Then he walked out of the doghouse. Blanche followed him. He started to run. Blanche trotted along behind.

"Help!" shouted Space Dog. He ran out of the yard. Blanche was hard on his heels. He jumped over a hedge for the first time in his life. Blanche jumped the hedge easily.

Down the sidewalk they ran, Space Dog barely in the lead. They raced across driveways and even a street. Drivers honked their horns and slammed on their brakes.

"Sorry!" cried Space Dog. No one heard him because he was running too fast. And Blanche was still right behind him.

Space Dog didn't know it, but he was running toward Roy's school. School was just letting out.

Roy was walking home from school. He noticed one of his sneakers was untied. He knelt down to tie it. *That's all I need*, he thought. *I'll trip over my own shoelace just as I'm running away from Stanley.*

Just then, Stanley came up behind Roy. "Hey, Roy-Boy," he teased. "Shoe trouble? Let me help you." Stanley leaned over and pulled off Roy's sneaker.

"Hey! Give that back!" shouted Roy.

He hopped after Stanley on one foot.

Stanley was a lot taller than Roy. He dangled the sneaker over Roy's head. "Come and get it," he said. "It's right here."

Roy hopped and jumped. The shoe stayed just out of reach. Stanley thought it was funny.

Roy was about to cry. He tried to sound tough. "You'd better give me that shoe," he said. His voice sounded a little squeaky. "Or I'll...I'll sic my dog on you!"

Stanley just laughed. "You don't even have a dog," he said. "If you did, he'd be a little pipsqueak like you!"

Just then, Roy saw Space Dog running up the sidewalk toward him. *Just in time!* thought Roy. *Come on, Space Dog!*

Space Dog saw Roy at the same moment. *Just in time!* thought Space Dog. *Save me, Roy!*

Space Dog ran up and hid behind Roy. When Blanche saw Roy, she came skidding to a stop.

"Go away, Blanche," said Roy. "Go home!" Roy knew Space Dog didn't like Alice's poodle.

Poor Blanche. She didn't want to leave Space Dog. But at last she turned around and started home. This time her tail wasn't wagging.

Stanley looked at Space Dog. Space Dog was tired and out of breath. He was still hiding behind Roy's legs. "Is that your dog?" said Stanley. "He *is* a pipsqueak! I knew it!"

"Stanley, give me my sneaker!" said Roy.

So this is Stanley, thought Space Dog. He looked at the mean face. He looked at Roy's shoe. All of a sudden, he under-

stood. Stanley was bullying Roy again. He knew what he had to do.

Space Dog tried to growl. *"Garur, garur,"* he said. He walked toward Stanley and growled louder. *"Garur, garur."* Stanley didn't drop the shoe.

"Your little dog doesn't scare me," he said.

Space Dog growled again. *"Grrr!"* Then he nipped Stanley on the ankle.

"Ouch!" cried Stanley. He dropped Roy's shoe and held his leg. "Keep that dog away from me! He probably has rabies!" Stanley limped away as fast as he could.

Space Dog spit out some lint from Stanley's sock. "Blech!" he said. "That kid's feet stink!"

"Oh, Space Dog!" said Roy, hugging him. "You saved me! You're the best friend I ever had!"

"Aw, it was nothing," said Space Dog. "And anyway, I owed you. You saved me from Blanche."

Roy hugged Space Dog tighter. Space Dog didn't say anything, but he liked it. If it had been a doggy thing to do, he would have hugged Roy back.

9

Howling in the Backyard

For dinner that night, the Barneses had meatloaf. It was not Roy's favorite. It was not Space Dog's favorite either. It reminded him of dog food.

"Mom and Dad," said Roy. "From now on *I'll* feed Space Dog. I'm big enough to take care of him myself."

Mr. Barnes patted Roy on the back. "That's what I like to hear, son!" he said. "You're growing up."

Mrs. Barnes smiled proudly.

friends there. *I've never had a better friend than Roy,* he thought. *No one's ever tried harder to make me happy.*

The two stood quietly side by side, thinking. Finally Roy broke the silence. He could not stand the suspense any longer.

"How's your engine coming?" he asked.

"It's not fixed yet," said Space Dog. "But I think I'll stop working on it for now. I won't need it for some time."

"Does that mean you're not going to leave?"

"Leave?" said Space Dog. "And go back to Tzaxette?"

Roy laughed.

"She's worse than Stanley," said Space Dog.

Roy and Space Dog got ready for bed. Outside Blanche howled. Inside the two friends fell happily asleep, with pillows over their heads to keep out the noise.

It's a dog's life on earth!
But Space Dog puts up with it for his
new best friend, a human boy called Roy.

Read all the Space Dog books!

SPACE DOG AND ROY
When a spaceship crashes in his backyard,
Roy gets what he's always wanted—a dog of
his very own!

And coming soon. . .

SPACE DOG AND THE PET SHOW
Space Dog agrees to enter a pet show for
Roy's sake. But he didn't bargain on a beauty
makeover at Dottie's Dog Salon!

SPACE DOG IN TROUBLE
A weekend at Granny's for Roy and his parents means a vacation for Space Dog—until
he's dog-napped by the dogcatcher!

SPACE DOG THE HERO
Roy's dad insists that Space Dog guard the
house. But Space Dog is a hopeless watch-
dog—he can't even growl!

About the Author

NATALIE STANDIFORD has often wondered if animals aren't secretly smarter than we think they are. She's sure that *kids* know a lot more than adults think they do. When she wrote about Space Dog, she imagined that he'd feel the way a lot of kids feel—misunderstood.

Natalie has written several books about dogs, but at home in New York City she has a cat, Iggy. So far, Iggy hasn't inspired any books. But you never know...

About the Illustrator

KATHLEEN COLLINS HOWELL began drawing pictures at the age of four and went on to study art in college. Today she is an illustrator of many books for children.

Kathleen and her husband, Jack, live half the year in Buffalo, New York, and half the year in rural England.